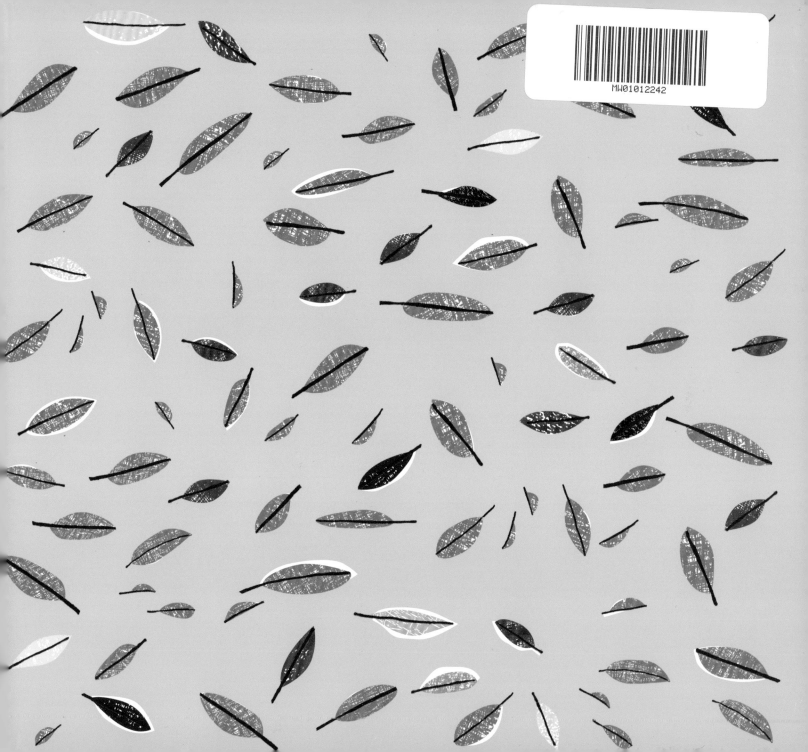

Chooky-Doodle-Doo

Jan Whiten   ILLUSTRATED BY **Sinéad Hanley**

CANDLEWICK PRESS

One little chooky chick
pulling at a worm.
Clucky cluck, worm's stuck.
What should chooky do?

Two little chooky chicks pulling at a worm.

Huffy puff, worm's tough.
What should chookies do?

Three little chooky chicks
pulling at a worm.
What's wrong? Worm's long.
What should chookies do?

Four little chooky chicks
pulling at a worm.
Pecky pick, worm's thick.
What should chookies do?

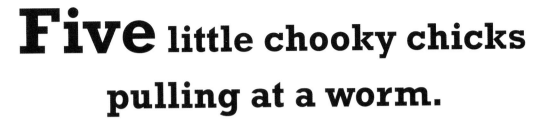

Five little chooky chicks
pulling at a worm.
Tug along, worm's strong.
What should chookies do?

Lots of little chooky chicks
and the rooster too
cannot get that stubborn worm—
cock-a-doodle-doo.

All the little chookies
with the rooster helping too,
might beat the squirmy wormy
if they form a chooky queue.

Now together, heave haul.
Pull harder, give their all.

Feathers fly, dusty squall.
Flap, flop—chooky sprawl!

Fancy that.
Who knew?
All that chooky-doodle-doo
for . . .

a farmer's buried shoe!
squawk!

For Uncle George,
who always wanted
a happy hen farm

J. W.

For Toby, Seth,
and Zachary

S. H.

First U.S. edition 2015

Library of Congress Catalog Card Number 2013957309
ISBN 978-0-7636-7327-7

14 15 16 17 18 19 CCP 10 9 8 7 6 5 4 3 2 1

Printed in Shenzhen, Guangdong, China

This book was typeset in Rockwell.
The illustrations were done in handcrafted and digital collage.

Candlewick Press
99 Dover Street
Somerville, Massachusetts 02144

visit us at www.candlewick.com

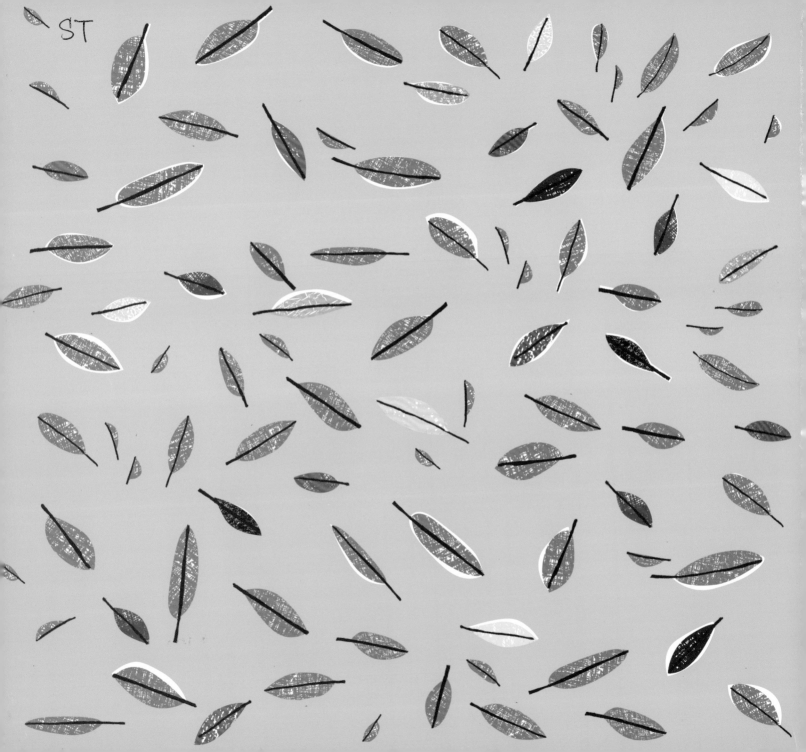